The Little Mermaid

REIMAGINED BY
Anna Kemp

ILLUSTRATED BY
Natelle Quek

PUFFIN

For the bold and beautiful Emily,
love Auntie Anna x

For my fincredible family,
and for James, my sole mate, *Natelle*

PUFFIN BOOKS

UK | USA | Canada | Ireland | Australia
India | New Zealand | South Africa

Puffin Books is part of the Penguin Random House group of companies
whose addresses can be found at global.penguinrandomhouse.com.

www.penguin.co.uk   www.puffin.co.uk   www.ladybird.co.uk

Penguin
Random House
UK

First published 2021
001

Text copyright © Anna Kemp, 2021
Illustrations copyright © Natelle Quek, 2021

The moral right of the author and illustrator has been asserted

Printed in China

The authorized representative in the EEA is Penguin Random House Ireland,
Morrison Chambers, 32 Nassau Street, Dublin D02 YH68

A CIP catalogue record for this book is available from the British Library

ISBN: 978-0-241-46982-8

All correspondence to: Puffin Books, Penguin Random House Children's,
One Embassy Gardens, 8 Viaduct Gardens, London SW11 7BW

MIX
Paper from
responsible sources
FSC® C018179

LONG AGO, deep beneath the ocean waves, there lived a little mermaid. She was the Princess of Corals and daughter of the Sea-King, but, more than anything, she was completely and utterly . . .

BORED.

Bored stiff.

So bored she wanted to yell
and pull her dark, foamy hair.
But yelling wasn't allowed.
Only singing.

And as for the hair, well that had to be combed: one hundred strokes in the morning
and one hundred strokes before bed. Because that's what mermaids do. But, with all
the singing and combing, combing and singing, the little mermaid did not have much
time to do anything else. Which was, of course, the point.

Every evening, the little mermaid and her two sisters had supper with their father. And every evening, the little mermaid would ask when she would be allowed to swim to the surface.

"Coral, my dear," the old Sea-King would sigh, shaking his seaweed beard, "the upper waters are dangerous. There are ships full of people. They drag nets behind them, big enough to snare whales. There's barely a living thing left up there."

Then he would get worked up and start stabbing the water with his fork.

"There is nothing so wicked and stupid," he'd growl, "as people! And if you think I'm going to let . . ." At which point Coral would stop listening. *People are wicked and stupid . . . giant nets . . . your poor mother!* She'd heard it a thousand times before.

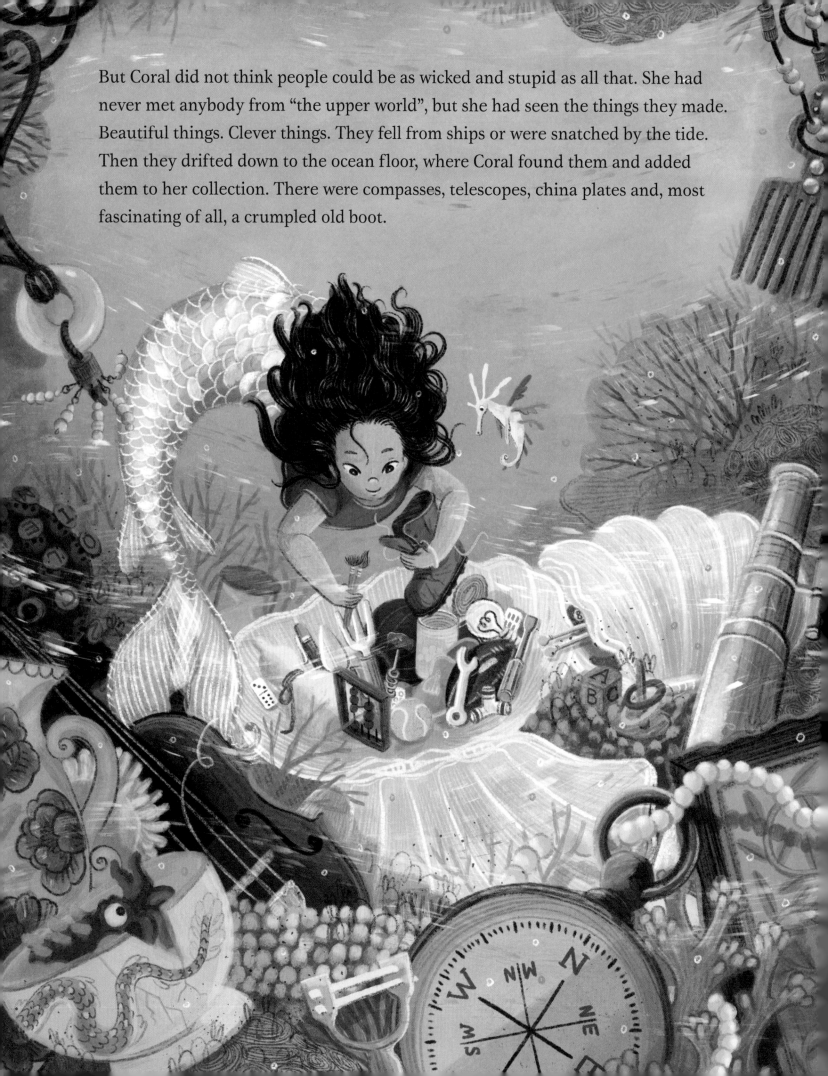

But Coral did not think people could be as wicked and stupid as all that. She had never met anybody from "the upper world", but she had seen the things they made. Beautiful things. Clever things. They fell from ships or were snatched by the tide. Then they drifted down to the ocean floor, where Coral found them and added them to her collection. There were compasses, telescopes, china plates and, most fascinating of all, a crumpled old boot.

"What do you think it's like to have feet?" she'd ask her sisters.

"I hear people run about like two-legged crabs," giggled Anemone.

"Yes!" added Periwinkle. "And when they get really excited, they hop from one foot to another. It's called 'dancing'!"

Then the sisters would flip about laughing. What strange animals people were. *Strange and brilliant animals*, thought Coral, gazing up through the crystal waters.

Then one day, Coral opened her treasure chest and gulped in shock. Everything had gone. All of it. She slammed the box shut and swished off to find her father.

"My little starfish," said the Sea-King, "you don't need that nonsense."

"But Dad!" Coral cried angrily. "They were my things!"

"You have plenty of other things!" The Sea-King laughed. "Combs of fine baleen, pearl necklaces, a whole stable of seahorses! Now off you float to your singing lesson. Madame Trout is waiting."

Coral pressed her lips tightly together as tears of rage mingled with the salty seawater. She didn't see the point of arguing. She already knew what she had to do.

Late that night, when the ocean was inky black, save for the blink
of neon jellyfish, Coral slid out of her sea-sponge bed and floated,
light as a bubble, towards the surface.

As she rose through the water, past pods of sleeping whales,
she felt her heart expand with joy.

Then she raised her head above the waves
and took her first gasp of air.

What she saw was beyond her imagining. The moon beamed, the stars glimmered and all was reflected on the sea below. A chill brushed the mermaid's wet cheeks.

"Wind!" She smiled and ducked back into the warm water. Then, with a twist of her body and a powerful flick of her tail, she leaped high out of the waves and arced through the air like a dolphin.

Night after night, the little mermaid stole out of her ocean bed and returned to the water's surface.

She saw wild swans, racing clouds and sky-splitting forks of lightning. But what really sent a thrill down her spine was the nearness of people.

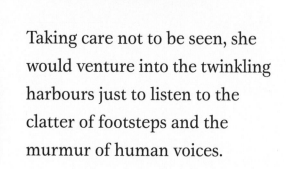

Taking care not to be seen, she would venture into the twinkling harbours just to listen to the clatter of footsteps and the murmur of human voices.

But as soon as the first flush of sunrise smudged the horizon, she raced home and tucked herself back into bed, snug as a pearl in its shell.

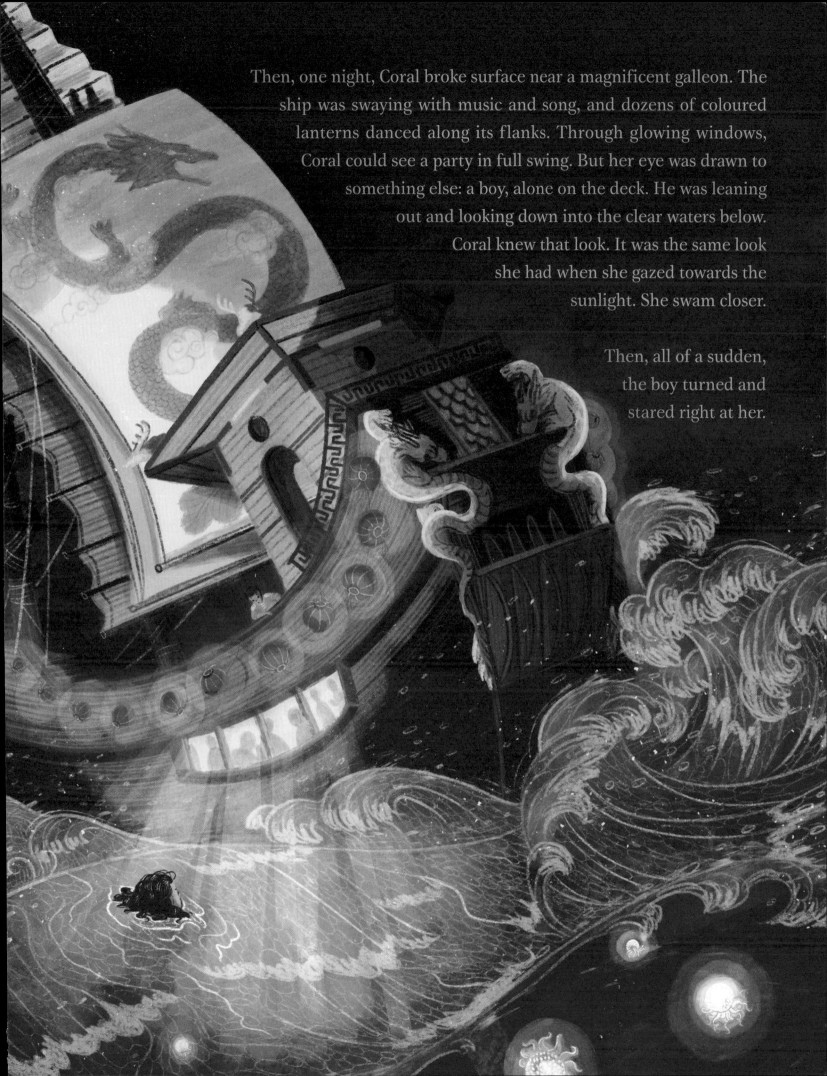

Then, one night, Coral broke surface near a magnificent galleon. The ship was swaying with music and song, and dozens of coloured lanterns danced along its flanks. Through glowing windows, Coral could see a party in full swing. But her eye was drawn to something else: a boy, alone on the deck. He was leaning out and looking down into the clear waters below. Coral knew that look. It was the same look she had when she gazed towards the sunlight. She swam closer.

Then, all of a sudden, the boy turned and stared right at her.

Coral dived quickly back underwater. As she hid beneath the waves, circling the
hull and wondering who the boy could be, she heard the ocean begin to growl.
A tempest was brewing. She darted to the surface to shout a warning, but the
wind was already up and the ship barely had time to unfurl its sails before
the waves rose, high and foaming all around.

The mermaid followed the galleon as it plunged and leaped across
the raging sea towards the harbour.

But the ship's timbers were creaking and groaning and, before it reached the shallows,
a giant wave swept the deck. Coral saw the boy flung into the swirling waters.
Bravely, she darted through the wreckage of the splintering ship. She was almost
crushed by a toppling mast, but she kept diving into the dark water, rising
and falling with the swells until, at last, she grasped a human hand.

The boy was limp and his eyes were closed. The mermaid used all her strength to hold his head above the surface till the storm passed and they could drift safely to shore. By the time she had left him on the sand, it was morning.

Coral waited in the shallows until she saw some fisherfolk race to his rescue. They rubbed his back as he spluttered back to life, then wrapped him tightly in a blanket and shouted for hot drinks to warm him.

Wicked and stupid? thought Coral as she swam back down to the ocean floor. *What nonsense! If only Dad could see what I see. If only he would listen.*

But the Sea-King was not in a listening mood.

"Dad's spitting clams!" frowned Periwinkle as Coral swam into the palace gardens.

"You'd better hide!" said Anemone. But it was too late. The Sea-King had grabbed Coral's tail in his huge barnacled fist.

"How could you be so foolish?" he bellowed, shaking with fury.

"But Dad!" pleaded Coral. "You're wrong about the upper world."

"You'll stay right here where you belong," her father growled. "It's time you learned to behave like a proper mermaid!"

"You can't keep me down here forever!" Coral wept.

But the Sea-King just folded his mighty arms and summoned his barracuda guard.

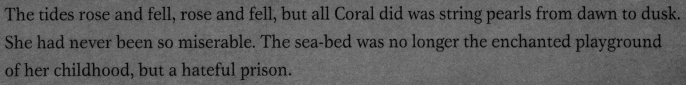

The tides rose and fell, rose and fell, but all Coral did was string pearls from dawn to dusk.
She had never been so miserable. The sea-bed was no longer the enchanted playground
of her childhood, but a hateful prison.

I don't want to be a "proper mermaid", she thought, whipping up the sand with her tail.
I don't want to be a mermaid at all.

There was just one person who could help her.
It was dangerous, no doubt. But her mind was
made up. So she hatched a plan, and waited for
her chance to slip away.

Coral shivered as she peered into the murk of the abyss. The deep ocean trenches were so far from the sun that even a mermaid's clear eyes could only see movement a few feet ahead. By which time it was too late. Down in the gloom lurked needle-toothed sea devils, red-eyed vampire squid, and hunting packs of wolf fish.

But, most monstrous of all, was the Sea-Witch.

Or at least, that's what people said. The Sea-Witch, they said, was neither of the sea nor of the land and, despised by all, had been cast into the depths, where she lived in a house of bones and ate small mermaids for breakfast. But people said a lot of things, and Coral preferred to decide for herself.

She might be a monster, Coral thought, *but she's my only hope.*

Then she slipped herself into a whirlpool

and was pulled down

into the cold,

cold deeps.

The Sea-Witch, who knew
everything, was waiting for her.

"So you want to be human," said a soft,
low voice. Coral could not see where
the voice came from but was aware
of tentacles twisting in the darkness.
"The price is high."

"I don't care," the mermaid replied,
"I can't live here a moment longer."
She glimpsed two shining, intelligent
eyes watching her through the gloom.

"The price," the witch continued, "is your voice. No singing, no laughing with your sisters and –" Coral felt sure the witch smiled – "no talking back to your father."

"I hate singing!" she blurted. Then felt a little foolish.

"The choice is yours, Coral. Think carefully."

But the little mermaid did not want to think. She wanted only to walk, run and dance on the shores above. She nodded impatiently and the witch set to work.

Coral's heart beat faster and faster as she spiralled to the surface, clutching a glittering vial of the witch's potion. As soon as she reached a secluded beach, she unstoppered the flask and drank the magic draught. It felt as if her body was being sliced in two. She opened her mouth to scream, but couldn't make a sound. Then she fainted dead away.

When she woke, a pair of curious eyes was looking down at her. Coral blinked in recognition. It was the boy from the ship.

"You haven't got any clothes on," said the boy, matter-of-factly. Coral looked down at her straight new legs, astounded. "Come on," he said, "before my mum and dad see you."

Coral tried to get to her feet but stumbled like a foal. The boy helped her stand and guided her up a lawn towards a shimmering palace.

"I'm Prince Eldoris," he said, "but you can call me Eldo. Who are you?"

Coral tried to answer but not a word would pass her lips.

For Coral, everything about the upper world was enchanting.

Carriage wheels, teapots, the insides of clocks – every detail glowed with magic.

Eldo, realizing she had nowhere to go, gave her a room in the vast palace

and, every day, they went for long, silent walks through the kingdom.

They climbed snow-topped mountains, rambled through sweet-scented forests –
and the light!

Oh, the light!

Coral's eyes had never seen so clearly and so far.

Every now and then, a gust of sea breeze reminded her of her family beneath the waves
and she felt a sudden swell of sadness. But she would push those feelings away, and let
her strong new legs take her wherever she wanted to go.

As for the prince's family, Coral did not
see them once. Indeed, the prince seemed
horribly lonely.

"Oh, my parents are always busy," Eldo
said one day. "They have to run the country.
Stuff like that."

Coral could hear the hurt in the
prince's voice and wished
she could comfort him.
But, to her frustration,
she couldn't utter
a word.

"I want to show you
something," said Eldo.

He led her up a winding
staircase to a room in the
tower. As the door swung open,
Coral's eyes widened in surprise.

"It's my collection," said Eldo, shyly. In shining glass cabinets were seashells of every colour, shape and size. "My parents think I should be out sailing and fishing like the other princes. But look at these!"

Eldo opened a drawer. It was full of pink-striped nautilus shells, fluted scallops and pearly green ormers.

"I found them on the beach," he said smiling. "Can you imagine how beautiful it must be on the ocean floor?" Coral bit her lip as she thought of her home in the sea. It was; it was beautiful. The prince picked up a spiralled conch and put it to her ear.

"You can hear the waves!" he smiled. Coral listened to the soft roar of the ocean, and felt a pain much sharper than the witch's potion.

The weeks became months and the trees turned from green,

to gold,

to frosted white,

and back again.

Now that he was no longer alone,
Eldo began to talk more, smile more.
He reminded Coral of a hermit crab,
emerging from its shell.

But, however much she loved her friend, Coral could not ignore the ache in her own
heart. She walked and ran and danced until her new feet were blistered and sore. But
however far she travelled, however high she climbed, the pain inside her did not lessen.

That spring, the theme of the royal carnival was 'Under the Sea'. Eldo was ecstatic but Coral felt uneasy as she watched the parade of papier-mâché narwhals, lobster puppets and, finally, enthroned on a giant scallop shell, a singing, sequinned mermaid.

"I thought I saw a mermaid once," said Eldo as the mermaid combed her long blonde wig. Coral's eyes widened. She wanted to tell him that yes, yes he did! But, as always, the words stuck in her throat.

"But my dad says mermaids don't exist." Eldo shrugged.

"I suppose he's right."

Suddenly, Coral was overcome by a great wave of despair. She wanted to shout that mermaids **did** exist: her sisters existed, her father existed, she existed! But she was trapped in her voiceless body – a body that wasn't even her own.

Eldo stared after Coral, bewildered, as she stormed off through a cloud of chiffon jellyfish.

That night, Coral crept down the moonlit lawns to the shore. Huddled on a rock near the shallows, she stared out on a sea that seemed as dark and solid as granite.

Salty tears rolled down her cheeks and great, silent sobs shook her body. How she longed to go home.

Then, just as she thought she would dissolve with grief, she saw ripples in the water.

It was Periwinkle! And Anemone!

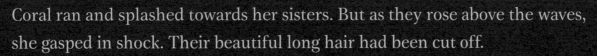

Coral ran and splashed towards her sisters. But as they rose above the waves, she gasped in shock. Their beautiful long hair had been cut off.

"We sold it to the witch," said Periwinkle, "in exchange for this!" She held up a gleaming vial.

"It will turn you back into a mermaid!" Anemone grasped Coral's arm. "But you must take it before sunrise! Now!"

Coral seized the potion and was about to gulp it down when something snagged in her mind. She looked back towards the palace. A single lonely light glowed from the prince's window.

"You must come with us," Periwinkle urged. "Come home. Please!"

Coral looked from the land to the sea, the sea to the land. The first red streaks were in the sky and she did not know what to do.

Then, like a fish through water, an idea flashed through her mind.
She gestured to her sisters to wait and ran to find the prince.

"What's the hurry?" asked Eldo as Coral dragged him down to the shore. But there was no time to waste. As soon as Coral's feet touched the water, she sipped the potion and, to Eldo's astonishment, transformed into a silver-tailed mermaid.

"It's you!" the prince gasped. "You saved me from the sea!"

"And you saved me," the mermaid croaked, her throat sore and scratchy. "But now I have to go home. Will you come with me?"

The mermaid offered the remaining potion to her friend.

Eldo sat down next to her on the sand. He looked out at the vast ocean, then back towards the palace.

"I can't," he said.

"But Eldo!" cried the mermaid. "You'll love it – the colours! The corals!"

"I know," said Eldo. "But this is my home."

Coral nodded. She knew he was right.

"Besides," the prince said smiling, "we're friends, aren't we? You can visit, teach me how to dive." His eyes brightened, "And you can tell me all about life under the sea! Oh, I knew mermaids were real!" he laughed. "I knew it!"

The little mermaid flung her arms around the prince and held him tight.

Then she slipped back
into the water
with her sisters and
spiralled down into
the deeps.

But her father only wept with joy. He rushed to Coral and pressed her to his great galleon chest.

"My little mermaid!" he cried.
"How I've missed you!"
"I missed you too, Dad," whispered the little mermaid.

At supper that evening, Coral told her family about the wonders of the upper world. She told them about the sound of wind through leaves, the beauty of fire, and the ingenuity of clocks. And she told them about Prince Eldoris: his kindness and his love of the ocean. The Sea-King chewed thoughtfully on his whelks, and he never called people wicked or stupid again.

From that day on, Coral freely roamed the oceans and would often visit Eldo in the lagoons and shallows of his kingdom.

She taught him about the sway of the tides,

the fragility of reefs,

and the ancient songs of the mer-people.

And when, a few years later, the prince became King, there began an era of great friendship between the peoples of the land and sea. When tempests raged, the mermaids would guide ships safely to shore and, in gratitude, the sailors never again let great nets drag the ocean.

And the Sea-Witch?

She watched it all with her great, glowing eyes.

And she smiled.